TRUBLOFF

The Mouse who wanted to play
the Balalaika

written and illustrated
by
John Burningham

Random House
New York

First Random House Edition 1965

© Copyright, 1964, by John Burningham

All rights reserved under International and Pan-American Copyright
Conventions. Published in New York by Random House, Inc., and
in London, England, by Jonathan Cape Limited

Library of Congress Catalog Card Number: 65-18166

Manufactured in the United States of America

TRUBLOFF

The Mouse
who wanted to play
the Balalaika

This is a picture of the Trub family,
and here is a story about one of the
mice, whose name was Trubloff.

Trubloff was born at an inn. The inn was part of a little village in Central Europe, where the winters were very cold and snowy.

He lived with his father, mother, sisters and brothers in a house which they had made behind the panelling of the Parlour Bar.

On most nights there were musicians in the Parlour Bar — gypsies who wandered from village to village, playing at the inns. In return they received food, drink, and sometimes money.

Trubloff used to sit and listen to them playing, often until it was long past his bedtime.

Then his mother would have to come and look for him. "You're a naughty mouse, Trubloff. You're never in bed when the others are," she would tell him. "But I love to hear the music, and watch the gypsies play," he would say. He was nearly always the last young mouse in bed and was often scolded by his parents, but when his mother came for him, he had to go.

One evening, Trubloff went to see old Nabakoff, the craftsman mouse, who asked him why he was always listening to the music. "Because I love it," said Trubloff. "Well," said Nabakoff, "I'd better make you a balalaika." Trubloff was overjoyed.

Old Nabakoff told him that he would have to wait for two or three days. Impatiently Trubloff paced up and down, day and night.

Now the innkeeper had been kept awake by the noise that the Trubs made with their scuffling and chattering. (Trubloff was one of the noisiest.) He had tried to make his old cat go after them, but the cat was not really interested, because he got plenty of food from the customers in the Bar.

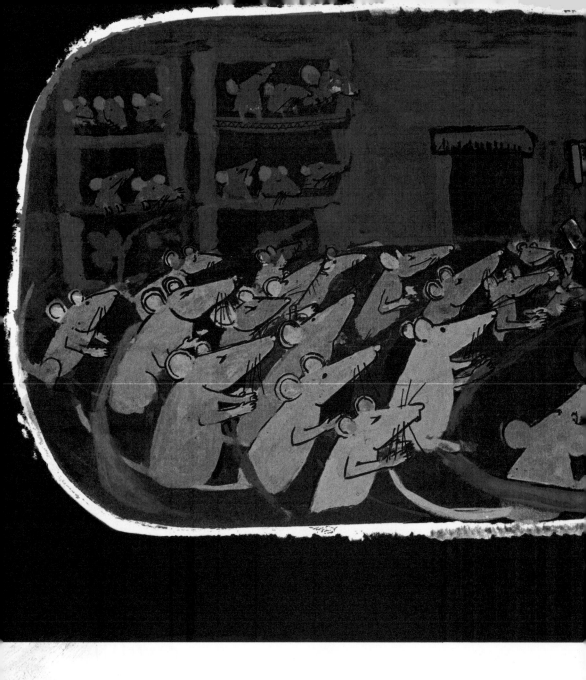

When Trubloff finally went to bed, he dreamed that he was the greatest balalaika-player in the whole country. In his dream, the

conductor of the orchestra stood humbly back while the audience
clapped and clapped. They could not have enough of his playing.

Nabakoff finished the balalaika and gave it to Trubloff, who rushed off to a corner where he could not be heard. But he found that playing the balalaika was not easy.

In the Bar one evening, an old gypsy, who was himself playing the balalaika, heard the strange noises coming from Trubloff's instrument. He looked down and saw Trubloff. "Hello, mouse," he said. "So you want to be a musician, do you?" Trubloff replied that he did. "Let's have a look at you," said the gypsy. Trubloff nervously went over, carrying his balalaika. "It's a pity," said the old man. "I could have given you lessons, but we are leaving tonight." Trubloff was very disappointed.

But then he had an idea: he would hide in one of the gypsies' sleighs and travel with them.

He did not dare to tell his parents. He knew that they would never agree.

He took his warm coat, some food, and, of course, his balalaika, and when he thought nobody was looking, he found a good hiding-place in one of the sleighs.

The gypsies said goodbye to the innkeeper, and then they were off, travelling into the night.

As soon as they were some distance from the village, Trubloff cautiously came out from the old gypsy's pocket into which he had climbed as the sleigh sped over the snow.

The old man was very surprised to see him, but when Trubloff reminded him about the lessons, he remembered, and said that he would teach him to play.

The gypsies travelled from inn to inn, playing and dancing. Trubloff always listened to the music and the old gypsy gave him lessons. He was learning quite fast, and the old man was pleased with his little pupil.

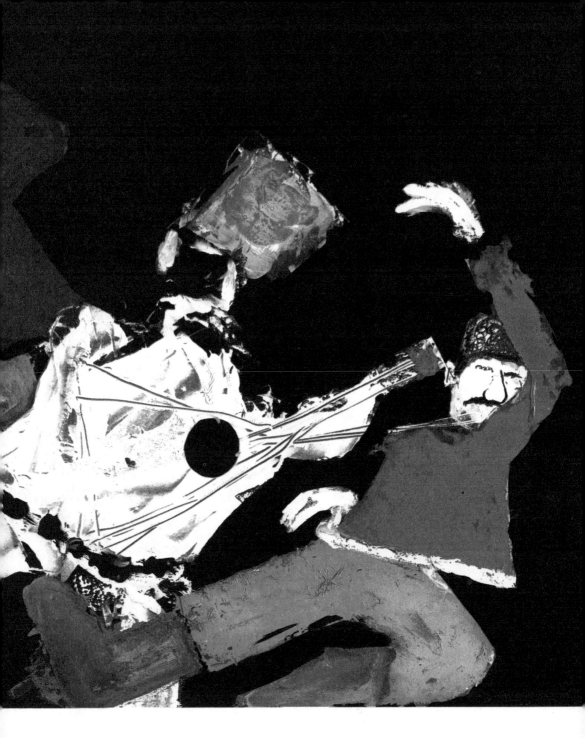

Now the Trub family had looked in vain for Trubloff, and Mrs. Trub became ill with the strain of it all. But then an old water rat told them that he had been seen leaving with the gypsies, and one of Trubloff's sisters bravely volunteered to go out and make a search.

Meanwhile the gypsies travelled on.

One night, while the gypsies were shelter-
ing in a barn, Trubloff's sister arrived on skis.
All the gypsies were asleep except for the old
man, who was giving Trubloff a lesson. Trubloff was startled to see his sister. "You must
come home at once," she said. "Our mother
is very ill."

She had brought with her an extra pair of
skis for Trubloff so that they would be able to
travel home much faster.

The two mice said goodbye to the old gypsy, and set off towards home on their skis.

At night they stayed wherever they could find the best shelter. Sometimes they had to curl up in the snow and sleep as best they could, but on other nights they were able to build a little fire.

Then came a terrible day when they were caught in a blizzard. This frightened them so much that they wondered whether they would ever get home to see their mother.

But the next day the sky was clear, and they
felt sure that, over the next hill, they would find
their own village.

At last they arrived and rushed up
to their mother's room. Both parents
were so overjoyed to see Trubloff

home, safe and sound, that they were not as severe in their scolding as they would otherwise have been. But Trubloff had to promise that he would not run off again without telling them.

Now in spite of their joy at Trubloff's return, Mr. and Mrs. Trub were still very worried. They had heard that the innkeeper was going to bring in some fierce farm cats to drive them and their children out of the inn. Mr. and Mrs. Trub did not know where they would go.

But on that very same evening, the innkeeper was in difficulties. The musicians who were to have played at the inn had not arrived, and the customers in the Parlour Bar were becoming impatient.

Trubloff had an idea. He went as close as he dared to the innkeeper and asked if he might be the musician for that evening. The innkeeper was amazed to see a mouse with a balalaika, but he had to admit, after hearing him, that Trubloff played well.

The innkeeper was so pleased with Trubloff that he told the Trubs they could stay on at the inn for as long as they wanted.

Mrs. Trub soon recovered from her illness now that her worries were over.

Trubloff's brothers and sisters learned to play instruments too. They formed a little band and often played in the Bar. Customers travelled great distances just to come and hear his music, and Trubloff's band became famous.

Now nobody knows exactly where to find the little inn which has a mouse band playing in the Parlour Bar.

But if you were to see a mouse on skis, it might well be Trubloff, and if you were to follow him, you might find the inn.

THE END

"Dearest Petunia," said Raccoon, "I must tell you something. Do you know why I asked you to come into the woods?"

"Your aunt!" cried Petunia. "Your aunt, we forgot her!"

"Oh, well . . . never mind," said Racoon. "What I must say is *thank you*, dearest Petunia, for saving my life.

From now on, I will be your truest friend, for ever and ever."

They chattered happily all the way back to Petunia's farm. When they parted company at the gate, Petunia said, "Really, Raccoon, it's the loveliest walk I have ever had, even if we never saw your aunt."

"Good-by, Petunia," said Raccoon. "I love you."

They fled through the meadow with the farmer after them.
But they soon lost sight of him.
He could neither run like a raccoon nor fly like a goose.
It was only in the middle of the forest
that Petunia and Raccoon stopped to rest.

"Oh, it's the end of me, Petunia," cried Raccoon.
"Look, the farmer has seen us; he is coming. Oh, Petunia."
But Petunia was already trying to open the door.
She shook it every possible way, tugging at it from all sides,
while the farmer was getting nearer and nearer.
Just as he reached them,
Petunia opened the door,
and Raccoon rushed out, free.

He sat Petunia on the smaller end
of the plank, under a low branch
of the tree. Then he climbed up
to a higher branch above the
other end. "Now, watch me,"
he said. "I'll jump down onto
the plank and you will go up,
up, up. . . ." Then he added to
himself, "And you will hit the
branch above, bang! and be
all muddled up."
Raccoon jumped,

but the plank yielded only a little
and sprang right up, throwing *him* back to the high branch
which *he* hit with *his* head . . . BANG!
"What happened?" shouted Petunia. "I didn't go up at all!"
"I did, didn't you see, you silly goose?" grunted Raccoon, rubbing
his head with one paw while he held on to the branch with the other.
"That's the wrong sort of seesaw.
Let's go find something else."

Raccoon was so tired and hungry now,
he only wanted something to eat. Anything!
The two walked on down the path. It led past a farm
which stood in the meadow at the edge of the forest.
"I think I smell raspberry jam," said Petunia.
"Strawberry," said Raccoon. "And, when all is said,
there is nothing better than strawberry jam in the morning.
I see it there in that wire box behind the barn."
Without stopping to think why strawberry jam should be there,
Raccoon rushed into the box. The door snapped shut.
The box was a trap.

"I have it—a seesaw,"
he cried presently, when
he saw a plank which
had been forgotten under
a tree by lumbermen.
The plank lay across
a stone with one end up.
"What's a seesaw?"
asked Petunia. "A very
amusing game," answered
Raccoon. "Let's play it."

After rubbing his paw and walking for awhile,
Raccoon forgot his pain and looked again
for a trick that would not fail.

and pushed him down to the forest floor.
His shrieks brought Petunia quickly to his aid.
"What have you done again, and what are you trying to do?"
she cried, seeing him walking on three legs.
"Ouch, my paw, that rock," muttered Raccoon.
"I made my wish, but it did not come true.
But it will *next time*," he added angrily.

Raccoon showed Petunia where she
must kiss the rock (low, very low
at the bottom), and he climbed to
the top to push the small rock onto
her head. As he pushed and pushed,
the rock rocked like a rocking
chair. But, instead of rolling toward
Petunia, it rolled back toward
Raccoon—

After Raccoon had cooled his head in a spring,
the two went on along the forest path.
Petunia picked leaves here and there
while Raccoon, hungrier than ever, looked about
for a proper way to trap the goose.
"THERE, the forest wishing stone," he suddenly cried,
pointing to a big rock with a smaller one on top.
"If you kiss the big rock at the bottom twenty times
and make twenty wishes, they will all come true."
"I don't think I can find twenty wishes," said Petunia,
"but I will try. Will you try, too?"
"I have only one wish," answered Raccoon, gritting his teeth.

Petunia chased the bees with her wings.

"There, dear friend," she said. "Stop running round and round.
Or run the other way. You make me dizzy.
Tell me, do the bees come from the other side of the world?"

"Don't stand there asking silly questions," growled Raccoon.
"Don't you see my head is all swollen?
Let's run before the bees come back."

He stuck his head into the hole to show Petunia.
"When *her* head is in the hole," he chuckled to himself,
"I will grab her neck and . . . ."
"Ouch! Ouch! Ouch!" he suddenly shrieked.
Backing out, he ran foolishly in circles
with a swarm of angry bees about his head.
He had put his nose into their nest!

Petunia giggled when Raccoon climbed back to the bank, dripping wet.
"Please don't mind my laughing, poor dear Raccoon," she said.
"But I never saw a dripping raccoon, and that's very funny."
"Not funnier than a giggling goose," grumbled Raccoon.
"Let's go on with our walk."
They were soon in the deepest part of the forest
where stood the old oak tree with holes in its trunk.
"Is this where your aunt lives?" asked Petunia.
"Why, no," answered Raccoon. "It's the magic tree of the forest.
When you put your head into the bottom hole,
you see the other side of the world,
where elephants climb trees and tigers ride camels."

But the tree, too rotten for their weight, broke in two
and crashed into the stream.
Petunia, with two beats of her wings, flew to the bank
while Raccoon fell in the water with a splash.

"We shall cross on that tree, one behind the other," said Raccoon.
"You shall not wet your feathers, nor I my fur. After you, please."
"All goes well," he thought, as he followed Petunia.
"In the middle of the log, I will jump on her neck and . . . ."

Chatting and walking side by side,
Petunia and Raccoon came to a wide stream
which was bridged by a fallen tree.

"It would be rude of me to refuse. Pray, lead the way."
"To you the honor, dear Petunia. I'll walk behind you."
"If we walked side by side," said Petunia,
"it would make conversation more pleasant."
"As you will, lovely Petunia," agreed Raccoon.
"Let us be patient," he thought to himself.
"I can best trap her once we are in the forest."

"Dear Petunia," said Raccoon, who had thought of a wicked scheme,
"you are so pretty. I love you, Petunia.
It would make me so happy just to have your company
for a little walk in the forest.
Today, I am going to see my old aunt. Won't you come along?"
"You are so polite and kind, Raccoon," said Petunia.

Raccoon's dreams had made him so hungry
that he went to Petunia's barnyard one morning,
at a time when all raccoons are asleep in their tree holes.

But what could he do? Petunia was stronger than Raccoon.
A blow from her wing had put to flight bigger animals than he.

Petunia did not know it,
but Raccoon thought of her every day,
and dreamed of her every night.
"How I long for Petunia," he sighed, "so handsome and so fat.
To think that I waste my time hunting mice and grasshoppers,
when I could feast like a king on a goose."

To Danielle

L.C. Catalog card number: 65-21559

This is a Borzoi Book. Published by Alfred A. Knopf, Inc.

PETUNIA,
I LOVE YOU

WRITTEN AND ILLUSTRATED BY

Roger Duvoisin

ALFRED·A·KNOPF : NEW YORK